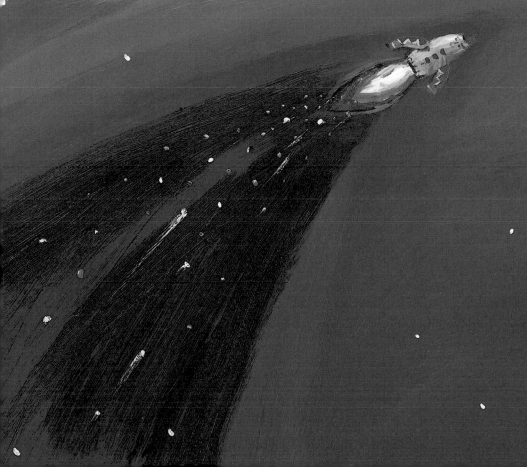

ROBBIE
THE ROCKET

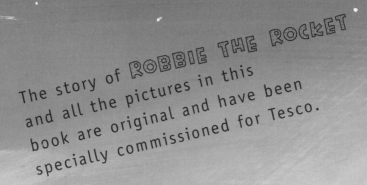

The story of ROBBIE THE ROCKET and all the pictures in this book are original and have been specially commissioned for Tesco.

Published by
Tesco Stores Limited
Created by Brilliant Books Ltd
84-86 Regent Street
London W1R 5PA

First published 2000

Text and Illustrations © 2000 Brilliant Books Ltd
Printed by Printer Trento S.r.l., Italy
Reproduction by Graphic Ideas Studios, England

fun to learn
collection

ROBBIE
THE ROCKET

Written by
Sophie Cox

Illustrated by
Christopher
Gilvan-Cartwright

Just before you go to bed at night,
have a look at the sky.

Does it look big, black
and empty...?

Well, it's not. Because
ROBBIE THE ROCKET
and his friends are up there,
working away while you sleep.

And far out
in deep, deep space,
an exciting adventure
is just about to happen...

ROBBIE THE ROCKET'S
radio crackled. It was
STELLA THE SATELLITE -
she sounded upset.

'Oh Robbie!...
awful happened!
...rock bashed me
...knocked off
main transmitter.
Hard...to do job
and pass on messages
...Space HQ
...going to get rid of me.'

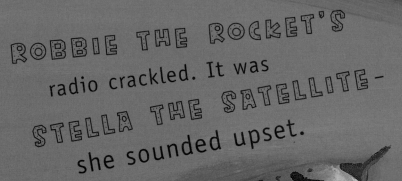

ROBBIE was upset. Poor STELLA.
He wanted to go and cheer her up,
but just then

another message came
through on his radio.

'Space HQ here.
There's...something
very strange...
on Mars.
Not like anything
seen before
...may be important!
Pick up... Space Rover
...investigate right away.'

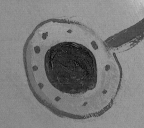

The message was very hard to understand.

'It's because Stella's been hurt and isn't working very well,' thought Robbie.

He went to pick up SPENCER THE SPACE ROVER from the Moon.

When he found SPENCER,
he touched down beside him,
lowered his ramp
and the little Space Rover
scurried on board.

ROBBIE told SPENCER
all about STELLA and about
the important job
they had to do on Mars.

As they zoomed through space
another message came over
from SPACE HQ.

'...blue
...at the foot...
large volcano...'

The message
was very crackly.
ROBBIE asked them
to say it again but there was
just a terrible hisssss.

'Oh well,' said Robbie.
'We'll just have to
do our best.'

He wasn't quite sure
what they were looking for
or where he should land,
so he looked out for a large volcano
and when he saw one, he lowered himself
on to the planet's rocky surface.

Mars looked hot, but in fact
it was very cold.
'Brrr!' Robbie said.
'Brace yourself, Spencer –
it's pretty chilly out there!'

SPENCER had never been
to Mars before
and was a little bit nervous.
But he bravely went outside anyway
and looked around
with his zoom lens.

ROBBIE watched SPENCER trundle away.
His radio was crackling again.
It was STELLA, but she sounded very faint.

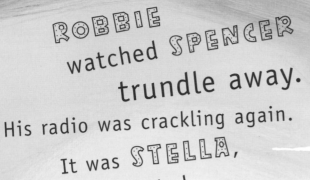
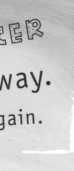

'...big...
...danger...
...immediately!'

Oh dear!
ROBBIE was worried.
STELLA was trying to warn him about something –
it must be very important.
He wondered what she was trying to tell him.

Suddenly,
something hit ROBBIE'S fuel tank!
'Ouch!' he said.
Then something else hit one of his fins.
'Ow!' cried Robbie looking around.

There was a shower
of little rocks
raining down on him.

Then ROBBIE saw something
that made him tremble
from his nose-cone
to his boosters.

From far away
something huge
was rushing towards him.

'Oh no! It's a comet!'
he gasped.
'And it's heading
straight for us.'

In fact, it was heading
straight for SPENCER!
ROBBIE tried to call him on his radio,
but he couldn't get through.
ROBBIE had to try and save him
before it was too late.

He blasted off, just as another
rock bounced off him.
Things were getting
really dangerous!

SPENCER spotted something blue.

'That must be it!' he thought,

just as he heard

ROBBIE'S engines roaring overhead.

'Whatever is he doing?'

Spencer wondered.

He didn't even notice the comet,

which was getting closer

all the time!

ROBBIE circled round and round
looking for somewhere to land,
but it was so rocky!
He'd have to take a chance... Crash!

He landed beside SPENCER.

'Quick Spencer!' he yelled.
'There's a comet heading
straight for us.

We've got to
get out of here!'

SPENCER
looked up to see the huge comet.
He gulped.
But he didn't want to give up,
and he started tugging
at the strange blue object.

'Leave it!' cried Robbie.
'There's no time, Spencer! Hurry!'
SPENCER gave one final tug and
suddenly the thing came free!

At last SPENCER
turned and raced
towards ROBBIE.

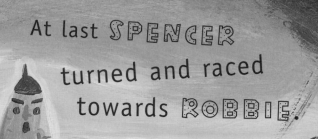

He went so fast that he
almost turned over!

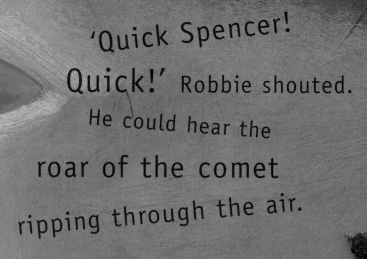

'Quick Spencer!
Quick!' Robbie shouted.
He could hear the
roar of the comet
ripping through the air.

SPENCER
zoomed up the ramp
and ROBBIE took off
before the door had even closed.

ROBBIE swerved away
from the comet, just as
there was a terrible...

EXPLOSION!

The comet had hit Mars!
They'd only just made it!

'Phew! That was close!'
Robbie said.
'Are you OK, Spencer?'
'I think so,' said Spencer,
trying to turn himself
the right way up.

'At least we got what we went for!' Spencer said.
'And do you know what it is, Robbie?'
'No idea!' said Robbie.

'It's Stella's transmitter!
She's going to be fine after all!'

And when ROBBIE and SPENCER gave STELLA her transmitter back, she was so happy she sent a message straight to SPACE HQ.

'Transmitter back in place, over. Business as usual,' she said proudly. 'Over and out.' And there wasn't a single crackle or hiss!